DATE DUE			
7-25	11/2		
4-17	7/6		
4-13	2/2		
7-9	7/24		
8-10	8/14		
3-4			
7 nov			
8/2			
8/10			
3/2			
5-19			

I Can Do It Myself

by Emily Perl Kingsley

Illustrated by Richard Brown

Featuring Jim Henson's Sesame Street Muppets

A SESAME STREET/GOLDEN PRESS BOOK
Published by Western Publishing Company, Inc.
in conjunction with
Children's Television Workshop.

I can put my toys away.

I can do it myself.

I can pour my juice.

I can button my buttons.

I can comb my hair.

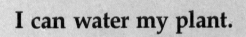

I can water my plant.

I can put on my boots.

I can write my name.

I can make my bed.

I can do it myself.

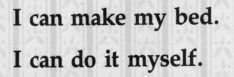

I can ride my tricycle.

I can set the table.

I can brush my teeth.

I can look at this whole book.

I can do it myself!